W9-BRS-996

PUPPY PATROL
TM
ORPHAN PUPPY

## BOOKS IN THE PUPPY PATROL™ SERIES

1. *TEACHER'S PET*
2. *BIG BEN*
3. *ABANDONED!*
4. *DOUBLE TROUBLE*
5. *STAR PAWS*
6. *TUG OF LOVE*
7. *SAVING SKYE*
8. *TUFF'S LUCK*
9. *RED ALERT*
10. *THE GREAT ESCAPE*
11. *PERFECT PUPPY*
12. *SAM AND DELILAH*
13. *THE SEA DOG*
14. *PUPPY SCHOOL*
15. *A WINTER'S TALE*
16. *PUPPY LOVE*
17. *BEST OF FRIENDS*
18. *KING OF THE CASTLE*
19. *POSH PUP*
20. *CHARLIE'S CHOICE*

PUPPY PATROL™

# ORPHAN PUPPY

JENNY DALE

Illustrations by Mick Reid

Cover illustration by Michael Rowe

AN
**APPLE**
PAPERBACK

SCHOLASTIC INC.
New York Toronto London Auckland Sydney
Mexico City New Delhi Hong Kong Buenos Aires

ISBN 0-439-33803-4



12 11 10 9 8 7 6 5 4 3 2 3 4 5 6 7/0

Printed in the U.S.A. 40
First Scholastic printing, November 2002

PUPPY PATROL
TM
ORPHAN PUPPY

# CHAPTER ONE

"Come on, Jake!" Neil Parker called to his young black-and-white Border collie as he tramped through the snow to the top of the ridge. He stopped to look back and laughed at Jake's antics. The young dog was racing back and forth, trying to catch the whirling snowflakes in his mouth. Below them lay the snowy roofs of the small country town of Compton.

"Hurry up!" Emily, Neil's ten-year-old sister, called impatiently from farther up the slope. "At this rate, the snow will have melted before we get to the top."

Neil laughed. "There's not much chance of that," he said as he ran to catch up with her, dragging his sled behind him. Neil had gotten up that morning to find a carpet of deep snow outside. It covered the yard and rooftops of King Street Kennels, the dog kennel and rescue center that his parents, Bob and Carole Parker, ran. It had continued to snow steadily all morning and Neil hoped it would last until Christmas, which was only a week away.

He gazed up at the sky, narrowing his eyes against the dancing flakes, then smiled with satisfaction. The clouds looked heavy and gray, and Neil was sure there was still plenty of snow to come.

"Come on!" Emily called again. "Everyone else is there already. We don't want to miss all the fun." She turned and hurried up the hill with her sled, her feet sinking into the snow with every step.

Neil whistled for Jake, then followed Emily, searching the hillside above as he walked. It was full of sledders and, even from this distance, Neil could identify quite a few of them. Chris Wilson and Hasheem Lindon, Neil's best friends from school, were trudging along the top of the ridge with a sled. Toby and Amanda Sparrow were there, too, with their young Dalmatian, Scrap. Steve Tansley, Neil's cousin, was having a snowball fight with a group of friends while his Labrador, Ricky, charged back and forth through the snow, barking with excitement.

"Look at Ben." Emily giggled as they climbed. "There's more snow on his coat than there is on the ground." Ben was the Old English sheepdog that belonged to Emily's best friend, Julie.

Neil grinned, then looked back at Jake again. The

collie was far behind but almost caught up with them. His fur was covered with snow, too. "Here, Jake," Neil called, bending down. "You look like a snow dog!"

Jake sped toward him, sending flurries of loose snow flying up behind him. He ran into Neil, knocking him over. "Get off!" Neil laughed, gently pushing the collie off him and jumping to his feet. He grabbed Jake's collar and brushed the worst of the snow off his coat while the Border collie nuzzled him with his wet nose. Neil gave him a dog treat from the supply he always carried in his pocket and Jake ate it eagerly. Then, with an excited bark, the young dog raced ahead up the hill.

"Here's the Puppy Patrol!" called Hasheem as Neil and Emily reached the top of the hill. He grinned at Neil. "Hey, haven't you got a special doggy sled for Jake to ride on?"

Neil laughed. "He refused to bring his own sled, Hasheem. He wanted to sit on your lap and ride down." He whistled and Jake came bounding up, ready to play.

"No way!" cried Hasheem, backing away in mock terror. Neil scooped up a handful of snow, shaped it into a snowball, and threw it at Hasheem. It hit his chest, leaving a snowy mark. Hasheem laughed and hurled one back, but his aim was off and he hit Chris instead. In seconds, a full-scale snowball fight had broken out.

"Is this a private fight or can anyone join in?" asked Julie, running up with Ben at her heels.

"The more, the merrier." Emily laughed, throwing a snowball at Julie and then diving out of the way as her friend tossed one back. Ben and Jake ran around wildly, leaping up to catch the snowballs as they flew over their heads.

"Yuck," Chris said after a while, brushing snow off his clothes so that it showered around his feet. "My gloves are soaked." He peeled them off and shook them out.

"Does anyone want a sled race?" Emily asked.

"You bet!" Neil exclaimed.

They all ran to get their sleds and lined them up

at the top of the slope. Jake and Ben watched with interest, and Neil began to wonder if Hasheem's suggestion that Jake should have a sled of his own wasn't such a bad idea, after all. The young Border collie would probably enjoy skimming down the hillside faster than he could run.

"Ready, set, go!" cried Neil, and they pushed off.

"Last one down has to give us all a piggyback ride to the top!" Julie shrieked as they raced downhill.

The ridge was perfect for sledding. The slope was long enough and steep enough for the sleds to build up speed, but it leveled out at the bottom so that it was easy to stop. As he zoomed down, Neil could hear Jake barking loudly behind him. But the Border collie couldn't keep up with the speeding sled and, when Neil glanced back over his shoulder, he saw Jake bounding after Ben instead, in a boisterous game of chase.

Julie reached the bottom of the hill first. Neil arrived seconds later, with Emily close behind. Chris and Hasheem were last, slowed down because they were sharing a sled.

"That was cool!" Neil cried, jumping up. "Let's do it again." He grinned at Chris and Hasheem. "Of course, as you two came last you'll have to give us all a piggyback ride to the top."

"No chance!" Hasheem yelled, already heading up the hill.

They walked back to the top of the hill, towing

their sleds and talking excitedly about Christmas. Jake and Ben ran over to meet them, barking greetings.

"Come on, Chris," said Hasheem. "If we get away quickly, we might win this time." He and Chris jumped onto their sled and sped away. Neil, Emily, and Julie quickly pulled their sleds into position. Jake gave an excited bark, then caught the rope of Neil's sled in his teeth. "Let go, Jake!" Neil said. "Do you want me to be last this time?"

Jake dropped the rope, then raced in circles around Neil's sled instead. By the time Neil was ready to go, Julie and Emily were already halfway down the hill and Chris and Hasheem were nearly at the bottom. "Typical!" Neil said, ruffling Jake's ears affectionately. Jake wagged his tail furiously and licked Neil's cheek.

"Move out of the way now, Jake," said Neil, gently shoving the Border collie to one side. He pushed off with his feet and sped away down the slope.

Suddenly, Neil saw a dark shape in the snow ahead of him, directly in his path. He squinted through the snowflakes, trying to figure out what it was. Then he realized, and his heart lurched. It was a Labrador puppy and, from what he could see, it was not very old.

"Look out!" Neil yelled. Frantically, he dug his heels into the snow, trying to slow his descent, but the sled swept on as fast as ever, and the puppy didn't move. It watched, wide-eyed with fear, as Neil sped toward it.

Neil pulled on the rope. He had to change direction. If he hit the puppy, it would be badly hurt. The nose of the sled inched around. Neil jerked harder and the sled swerved to the left.

To his relief, he realized that he was going to just miss the puppy — if it stayed where it was. But now Neil was heading for a prickly holly bush. He jerked on the rope again. This time it was too late. Shutting his eyes and throwing up his arms to protect his face, he sped straight into the bush.

# CHAPTER TWO

The branches scratched Neil as he plunged into the holly bush, the prickly leaves tearing at his clothes. A branch caught in the collar of his coat and he fell into the snow.

He lay still for a moment, looking up at the dark glossy leaves and scarlet berries above his head. One of his gloves had been torn off in the crash and there was a long scratch on the back of his hand. Neil flexed his arms and legs, to make sure he hadn't broken any bones. Then he rolled over and sat up.

"Neil!" Emily's frightened voice reached him from the bottom of the hill. "Are you all right?"

"Neil!" Chris yelled. "Where are you, buddy?"

"Over here," called Neil. "I'm OK." He crawled out of the bush.

Jake dashed down the slope, sending snow sliding ahead of him. He stood in front of Neil and looked at him with curiosity.

"It's OK," Neil said, hugging the Border collie. "I'm not hurt."

Ben arrived a second later and plopped down in the snow beside Jake, his tongue lolling. Neil patted him, too.

Emily came charging up the hill, her face pink from running. Chris, Hasheem, and Julie were close behind. "Are you all right?" Julie asked anxiously.

"Fine," said Neil as he got to his feet. "Except for a few scratches and a lost glove, anyway. Is the puppy OK?" The Labrador was still standing above them on the slope, chest-deep in snow. It was watching them with huge brown eyes, its chocolate-brown coat speckled with snowflakes.

Hasheem laughed. "There's nothing wrong with you if you're worrying about dogs again!"

"The puppy looks OK," said Emily. "But why on earth is it here alone?"

"That's what I'd like to know, too," Neil said angrily. "It's too young to be out in weather like this." He set off uphill toward the puppy, with the others trailing after him. "The poor little thing must be frozen. I'd really like to hear what the owners have got to say about —" He broke off suddenly. "Hang on! Isn't it Holly, one of the Labrador puppies from the litter at the rescue center? It looks exactly like her. And it's the right size."

"It does look like her," Emily agreed, "though I'm not one hundred percent sure."

"What, she's one of those tiny puppies that were living in a box in your kitchen for a while?" asked Chris. "I fed one of them once when I came over to your house. It was a little black one."

Neil nodded. "That's right." The Parkers had hand-fed the four tiny Labradors after they were found abandoned in the woods on the far side of Compton. They were only a few days old when they were found, and they had lived in the kitchen until they were big enough to move into the rescue center.

"I fed them a couple of times, too," Julie said. "They were really sweet." She looked at the puppy again. "Are they all as big as this one now?"

"One of the black ones, Santa, is a little smaller," said Neil. He signaled to everyone to slow down as they got closer to the Labrador puppy. It was important to approach her quietly so they didn't frighten her. He placed a restraining hand on Jake's collar. "Can you hang on to Ben, Julie?" he asked.

Julie grabbed hold of the Old English sheepdog.

"Someone left the puppies to die," Emily explained to Hasheem. "The owner dumped them in a bag in the middle of nowhere."

"That's terrible!" said Hasheem angrily. "What an awful thing to do!"

"They could easily have died from the cold," Emily went on with a shiver.

"Or starvation," Neil added with a frown.

"I can't imagine anyone being that cruel," said Chris.

"We don't get many cases as bad as that," Emily said. "And luckily, the puppies were found very quickly by a man who was out walking his dog. He brought them right over to King Street Kennels."

"The Puppy Patrol to the rescue again!" Hasheem said. "What on earth would dogs do without the Parkers and their rescue center?"

"Wait here, now," Neil said over his shoulder. "The puppy will be scared if we all get too close." He clipped on Jake's leash and thrust it into Emily's hand. "Stay, Jake," he told the Border collie. Then he inched forward cautiously so that the Labrador wouldn't run off. "Holly," he called softly.

"Holly! Very appropriate," Hasheem joked, "since you've just wrecked a holly bush, Neil, with your crazy sled run."

They all started to laugh, but Neil turned and placed a warning finger on his lips. "Don't scare her," he whispered, and the laughter quickly died away. "Holly," Neil called again. "Here, Holly. Good girl."

At the sound of her name, the Labrador puppy pricked up her ears and wagged her tiny tail feebly.

"I *knew* it was Holly," said Neil.

"Julie and I will get the sleds while you get a hold

of Holly," Emily said. "We'll take Jake and Ben with us, just in case they bother her. Come on, you two, let's go," she called to the dogs.

Holly watched Neil with a trusting expression as he came toward her. At last he was close enough to touch her. He reached out a hand, letting her sniff his bare skin, then he lifted her into his arms. "Good girl," he said soothingly.

The puppy snuggled against him, shivering. "Poor thing, you're frozen," said Neil, brushing snow off Holly's glossy coat. She was wearing a red leather collar with a name tag. Neil twisted the collar around until he could read the tag. The name *Morgan* was on it, with a telephone number underneath.

"Is it definitely Holly?" Chris asked, moving forward and holding out his hand to the young Labrador. She stretched forward to sniff him, then sank back against Neil's chest again with a weary sigh.

"Yes." Neil unzipped his coat and tucked the shivering pup inside. "It says Morgan on her name tag. That's the name of the people who adopted her."

"Is she going to be all right?" asked Chris, gently stroking her chin with one finger. Holly twisted her head and licked his glove with a tiny pink tongue.

Neil was relieved to feel her tail thud against his chest — she was obviously feeling better already. "She's just cold, scared, and worn out," he said. "But she'll be fine when she's warmed up and rested."

Emily and Julie climbed up the hill, pulling the sleds. Jake was off his leash now and was carrying Neil's missing glove in his mouth. He dropped it at Neil's feet, then sat down proudly, his wagging tail sweeping the loose snow from side to side.

"Well done, Jake," Neil praised. He felt in his pocket for a dog treat but the bag wasn't there.

Emily laughed. "I don't think Jake should have any more treats. He found the bag under the bush while he was searching for your glove and gobbled down most of them!"

"Ben helped." Julie giggled.

Neil grinned and patted the Border collie's head. Then he pulled the glove on gratefully, suddenly realizing how cold his hand was.

"What are we going to do with her?" asked Emily, petting Holly's ears.

Neil searched the hillside. "Nobody seems to be looking for her, so we'd better take her back to her home. Her owners live in one of those old cottages that back up to the ridge. I remember thinking it was an ideal place for a dog —" He broke off, frowning. Once again, he tried to imagine what sort of people would let a young puppy wander off alone in the snow. His mom and dad always checked that rescue dogs were going to good homes, but maybe they'd made a mistake this time. . . .

"Have you found homes for the other Labrador puppies?" asked Julie as they walked along the ridge. She stroked the top of Holly's head, and Neil felt the puppy's tail wagging again inside his coat.

"No, the other three are still at the rescue center," he said.

Julie frowned. "You'd think lots of people would want to adopt gorgeous little creatures like this."

Holly gave a tiny high-pitched bark, as though she'd understood what Julie said and fully agreed.

"I'm sure we'll find homes for the others soon," said Neil. "I want to see them all settled by Christmas."

Chris whistled. "Do you think you'll do it? Finding

homes for three puppies in a week is pushing it a little, isn't it?"

Neil squared his shoulders determinedly. "We'll do it."

They reached the end of the ridge. Low-roofed, old-fashioned cottages were clearly visible through the leafless trees ahead. Neil and Emily said good-bye to Chris, Hasheem, and Julie and set off down the narrow path that led between two of the cottages, to the quiet road beyond. Jake and Ben touched noses, then Jake trotted quickly after Neil.

It didn't take long to find Ridgeview Cottage, the Morgans' house. Neil marched up to the front door and rang the bell, with Emily and Jake close behind.

A plump, anxious-looking woman opened the door. "Mrs. Morgan?" Emily asked politely.

The woman nodded. "That's right." Suddenly, she caught sight of the puppy peeking out from inside Neil's coat and her face lit up. "Holly! Thank goodness! We've been looking everywhere for you," she said before Neil had a chance to speak. She held out her hands and Neil placed Holly in her arms.

"It's all right, girl," he said soothingly. "You're home now."

"She is all right, isn't she?" Mrs. Morgan asked, concerned.

"She seems fine — just a bit scared," Neil said. "Er . . . why exactly was she out on her own?"

"I let her out in the yard," said Mrs. Morgan. "I

thought it was safe. When I went to get her a few minutes later, she just wasn't there. There must be a hole in the fence." She hugged the little puppy. "I've been so worried about her."

Mrs. Morgan invited Neil, Emily, and Jake inside. "Thank you so much for bringing her home," she said, leading the way into a large, welcoming kitchen at the front of the house. "My husband's still out searching for her — he'll be so relieved."

A log fire was burning cheerfully at one end of the kitchen, its flickering flames casting an orange glow across the floor. Mrs. Morgan crossed to a large closet and took out a fluffy pink towel. Then she sat down in a chair, cradled Holly on her lap, and rubbed her dry.

"Would you like to sit down?" Mrs. Morgan asked, smiling up at Neil and Emily.

They settled down on the big, comfortable sofa, while Jake lay down by the fire. Neil relaxed. He'd been angry with the Morgans for letting Holly roam free, but now it seemed that he'd made a mistake. Mrs. Morgan was clearly just as concerned about the Labrador as he was.

"She's a terrific little puppy," said Neil, watching the Labrador, who had curled up on Mrs. Morgan's lap and was dozing contentedly.

"Yes, Holly's going to be our daughter's dog," explained Mrs. Morgan. "We only moved here two weeks ago, and a few days before that our dog died." She sighed. "We'd had her for sixteen years and we all miss her badly, but our daughter, Alex, is heartbroken."

They heard a door open at the back of the house. "I can't find her anywhere," a man's worried voice called. "I've been all over the ridge but —"

"It's all right, John," Mrs. Morgan interrupted. "Holly's home. Some kind people brought her back." She turned to Neil. "How did you know where to bring Holly?"

"We recognized her and then saw your name on her collar," explained Neil. "Our parents own King Street Kennels, and I remember them saying that Holly's new owners lived here."

Mrs. Morgan smiled. "You must be Neil, then. Alex is going to be in your class at school. And you must be Emily. Your dad told me all about you two."

A tall, smiling man came into the room. He was still wearing his coat and hat and his face was red with cold. "What a relief!" He took off his gloves and patted Holly affectionately. She lifted her head and blinked at him, then fell asleep again. "Thanks for bringing her home. Where did you find her?"

"Up on the ridge. We were sledding there," said Emily. "In fact, we're going back there now. Do you think Alex would like to come with us?"

"It's nice of you to ask, Emily," Mrs. Morgan said.

"I'm sure she'd love to, but she's not here. She's been staying with her grandparents in Manchester since we moved, so she could finish the term at her old school." She glanced at her watch. "I thought they'd be here by now, though," she added. "Her grandmother's bringing her over. Perhaps the snow held them up."

"She doesn't know about Holly yet," explained Mr. Morgan. "But she'll be really excited when she meets her." As he spoke, a red car pulled up outside. "At last! Here they are," he said. "I'll go let them in."

Neil and Emily watched through the window as Alex and her grandmother came up the snowy path, each carrying a suitcase. Alex was tall and skinny, with long dark hair pulled back into a ponytail. She wasn't wearing a coat, and the falling snow speckled her black sweater. *She looks just like a Dalmatian in reverse,* Neil thought, grinning to himself.

Holly opened her eyes and sat up, refreshed by her nap. Mrs. Morgan put her down on the floor. "Alex is coming, girl," she said.

Holly wagged her tail and gave a tiny bark. Jake stood up, obviously intending to go and make friends with the puppy, but Neil told him to stay and the Border collie obediently sat down again.

Neil heard Mr. Morgan say hello to his daughter. "Go on into the kitchen, Alex," he continued. "We've got a surprise for you."

Alex appeared in the doorway, followed by her dad

and grandmother. "Hello, dear," said Mrs. Morgan, giving her a hug. "Meet Holly. She's your new dog."

Alex's smile faded. She stared at Holly in horror. "How could you? I don't want a new dog," she cried and burst into tears.

# CHAPTER THREE

"If I can't have Daisy, I don't want any dog." Alex sobbed. "Don't you understand that?"

"But Daisy's not with us anymore, sweetheart," Mrs. Morgan said gently. She tried to put her arms around her daughter, but Alex pulled away.

Holly trotted toward Alex, her tail wagging and her mouth open in a welcoming grin. "Look, she likes you already," Mr. Morgan said encouragingly.

Alex shook her head. "I don't want her. I'm never having another dog." She stumbled out of the room with tears pouring down her cheeks. Her grandmother followed, calling to her to come back.

Holly sat down suddenly and stared after Alex, whining. Neil was just about to go to her when Mrs. Morgan picked her up. "It's all right, Holly," she said reassuringly, stroking the puppy that nestled against her.

Neil knew how Alex was feeling. When his own dog, Sam, had died, he'd been devastated. But at least he'd had Jake, Sam's son, to ease the pain. He bent down to pet Jake, running his hand over the Border collie's coat and letting Jake nuzzle his neck. *It was never easy when a dog died*, he thought, *but in the end you had to move on.* There were so many other dogs needing a loving home.

"Oh, dear," said Mr. Morgan, staring after Alex in dismay. "What on earth are we going to do now?"

"I really don't know." Mrs. Morgan's shoulders slumped. "I was sure she'd fall in love with Holly the moment she saw her."

There was an awkward silence.

"Look," said Neil, "if you like, we could take Holly back to the rescue center — just for a little while."

The Morgans exchanged worried glances. "Perhaps it would be best," Mr. Morgan said hesitantly.

"She'll be back with her brothers and sister," Neil pointed out.

"And maybe Alex will change her mind," added Emily. "After all, how could she resist such a gorgeous little puppy?"

"I hope you're right," Mr. Morgan said.

Mrs. Morgan shook her head firmly. "I'm sure Alex will realize she wants her soon. She's probably thinking it over right now."

"But you know how stubborn she can be sometimes," Mr. Morgan reminded her.

Mrs. Morgan bit her lip. "I know. But poor Holly. She's such a lovely puppy. *I* don't like the idea of having to part with her." She hugged the Labrador tightly.

"We just need to give Alex some space," Mr. Morgan said. He reached out for Holly, and Mrs. Morgan handed her over reluctantly. "She may decide she wants to keep her in just a day or two," Mr. Morgan reassured his wife, "but it'll be best if Holly's not here reminding Alex of Daisy until she's used to the idea of having another dog."

Mrs. Morgan gave a weak smile. "I know you're right, John," she said. "But all the same . . ." She gave Holly one last pat, then turned to Neil. "I'll get her things." She hurried out of the room, returning a few minutes later with a dog carrier, a soft blue blanket, and a squeaky rubber bone.

Emily spread the blanket in the bottom of the dog carrier. "This will keep Holly warm on the way home," she said.

Neil took Holly from Mr. Morgan and put her in the carrier. "Good girl," he said as she snuggled into the blanket. He put the rubber bone beside her and shut the door, making sure the catch closed properly. "Don't worry. We'll take good care of her," he promised, as he stood up. He called Jake to heel and picked up the dog carrier. Then he, Emily, and Jake went back out into the snow.

"Thanks for all your help," Mrs. Morgan called after them.

Neil and Emily waved as they headed home. Emily pulled both sleds behind her while Neil carried Holly. "Poor thing," he said. "Let's hope Alex decides she wants her soon. If not, we're going to have to find homes for *four* puppies before Christmas!"

A gray car was approaching King Street Kennels when Neil, Emily, and Jake arrived home with Holly. "It's Gavin and Jet," Emily said. Gavin Thorpe was the young pastor in Compton, and Jet, his black Labrador, always stayed at King Street Kennels when Gavin and his wife, Susie, went on vacation.

"I wonder if he'd like one of the Labrador puppies to keep Jet company," said Neil thoughtfully.

Emily shook her head. "I don't think so. Susie's going to have her baby soon. I can hardly see her and Gavin wanting a baby *and* a puppy."

"Yeah, I suppose it would be difficult," Neil agreed.

The car came to a stop on the snowy driveway. Gavin climbed out and Jet jumped out after him. "Hello, you two. Lovely day," Gavin joked, looking up at the sky.

"Hello, Gavin," Neil and Emily said together.

Jet trotted toward them, tail wagging and eyes

bright. "Hi, Jet," Neil said, running a hand over his smooth fur. He put the dog carrier down, opened its wire door and lifted Holly out, still wrapped in her blanket. Jet stretched up to sniff her. She peeked out of her blanket, her dark eyes wary as she looked at the newcomer.

"It's OK, Holly," said Neil, giving her a comforting pat.

Emily bent down to hug Jet, and he licked her cheek affectionately. Then he turned to Jake. The two dogs touched noses briefly before launching into a boisterous game of chase, racing around and around Gavin's car and occasionally wriggling underneath it and out the other side.

"Have you come to book Jet for a vacation?" asked Emily.

"Not this time," said the pastor. Jet ran back to him and Gavin ruffled his glossy black fur. "Actually, I've come to ask your dad a huge favor."

"You'd better come in, then," Neil said. He and Emily led Gavin around the side of the house and into the kitchen. The house was warm and bright and smelled deliciously of spicy pumpkin pie. A Christmas song was playing on the radio.

Carole was bending over the kitchen table, rolling out pastry. Sarah, Neil and Emily's five-year-old sister, was helping her, squeezing pastry scraps into Christmassy shapes. "I'm making an angel and Santa Claus and a stocking," she said proudly, holding up one of the shapes to show them. Her eyes widened as Holly poked her head out of the blanket. "A puppy!" she squealed, delighted. Dropping the pastry, she hurried over to Neil.

Carole Parker looked up. "Hello, Gavin," she said. "Come and sit down while I see what Neil's up to." She shot Neil a questioning glance.

"Thanks," said Gavin. He unbuttoned his coat and sat down, while Jet settled contentedly at his feet.

Carole pushed a strand of dark hair out of her face with the back of one floury hand, leaving a white streak across her forehead. Then she turned to Neil. "Where on earth did you get that puppy?"

"It's Holly," Neil said gloomily, and he and Emily explained what had happened.

"You were right to bring her back." Carole sighed. She brushed flour off her hands, then came to look at the puppy. "I wouldn't like to think of her belonging to someone who didn't want her," she added, rubbing the side of the puppy's head with one finger. Holly stuck out a small pink tongue and licked Carole's hand. "Poor Alex. I can understand why she'd feel like that. It's very hard to lose a dog you love. But maybe she'll change her mind."

"I hope so," said Neil. He was sure Holly was just what Alex needed.

"We could keep Holly," Sarah said eagerly, stretching up on tiptoe to stroke the puppy. "She gets along with Jake and —"

"We are not having another dog," Carole said firmly.

"But she's really sweet —" wailed Sarah.

"No!" said Carole.

"Do you want us to put her back in the rescue center?" asked Neil. He wished they could keep Holly, but he knew it would be pointless to try to talk his mother into it.

"Yes, please," Carole said. As she turned to Gavin, Jake trotted across to her and rubbed against her leg, soaking her jeans. "Jake!" she groaned.

"Yeah, he's pretty wet from being out in the snow,"

said Neil. "Could you give him a rubdown, please? And can you make sure his feet are dry?"

Carole laughed. "I do know how to look after dogs, Neil."

Neil laughed, too. "Sorry."

In spite of the snow outside, the rescue center felt wonderfully warm when Neil and Emily went in. "I'll fix a bowl of food for her," said Emily. "She must be starving after being out in the cold for so long."

"Good idea," Neil said. He got a towel and gently rubbed Holly's head — the only part of her that had been exposed to the weather since she'd been out of the dog carrier. By the time she was dry, her fur was standing up in chocolate-brown spikes. Neil smoothed it down, then set the puppy beside the bowl of food Emily had prepared. She ate it hungrily.

When she'd finished eating, Neil carried her to the pen her sister and brothers shared. The puppies were in their basket, asleep in a contented heap. Holly whined and wagged her tail as she picked up their scent. The puppies stirred.

"Come on, you guys. Wake up and say hello to your sister," Neil called as Emily opened the door. The smallest puppy, a black Labrador they had named Santa, struggled out from underneath his heavier golden sister, Candy, and ran to the door. He eyed Holly inquisitively, his tail swinging from side to side.

Neil carried Holly into the pen and set her down. In seconds, the other three puppies, two black and one golden, were all around her, sniffing her, touching noses, and welcoming her home. Then the four of them began a wild and joyful game of chase.

Neil watched with mixed emotions. It was good that the puppies were glad to see Holly, but he couldn't help feeling sorry for her. The rescue center was warm and comfortable, but it wasn't nearly as nice as the Morgans' house. *She'll miss the attention that the Morgans have given her, too*, Neil thought. He made up his mind to visit her as often as he could.

Gavin, Carole, and Bob were talking and drinking coffee when Neil and Emily went indoors. Jake and Jet were lying by the stove. Jake jumped up and trotted across to Neil, leaping up to lick his face.

"Down, boy," Neil commanded.

Jake sat down obediently, watching Neil intently, his bright eyes sparkling.

"You've got him well trained," said Gavin with admiration.

Neil laughed. "Most of the time. But he has his moments, don't you, Jake?" The Border collie barked in response.

"Anyway, Gavin, can we do something for you, or is this just a social visit?" Bob asked.

"I need some help, I'm afraid," said the pastor.

Bob stroked his beard thoughtfully. "I'll help out if I can, but we're a bit pushed for time today. Bev and Kate aren't working, and this snow means that simple jobs take twice as long." Bev and Kate were King

Street Kennels' hard-working and committed kennel assistants.

Gavin nodded. "The snow's caused problems on the roads, too. I hope it's not going to take me too long to get home — I don't like leaving Susie on her own." He took a cell phone out of his pocket and made sure it was turned on. "She's going to call me if anything happens. The baby's due in ten days."

Carole smiled. "You must be really excited."

"I can't wait," Gavin said. "Our first son or daughter!"

"So do you want me to drive you both to the hospital in the Range Rover when the time comes?" asked Bob.

Gavin shook his head. "It's not that. It's a rather unusual favor, actually." Neil thought he looked slightly embarrassed. "You see, I'm going to set up a Santaland in the church hall — for children and dogs."

"That sounds super!" Neil cried.

Bob laughed. "A Santaland for dogs?" He put down his empty coffee mug. "It's an original idea — I'll give you that."

"We've got to raise some money to get the church hall roof repaired," said Gavin. "There are so many dogs in Compton, I thought that people might be willing to pay a small amount to bring their kids *and* their dogs to see Santa Claus."

"I'll bring Jake," said Neil. "He'll love seeing all his doggy friends." He ruffled the Border collie's ears and Jake's tail thumped rhythmically on the floor. "Lots of people will come. Doctor Harvey will bring Finn and Sandy —" Neil began.

"And Julie and Ben will come," Emily chipped in. "And Steve and Ricky."

"I bet Mrs. Jepson will bring Sugar and Spice," said Neil with a laugh. "In fact, she'll probably bring them four times at least." Sugar and Spice were the most pampered pooches in Compton.

"So where does Bob come into this?" asked Carole.

Gavin blushed slightly and twisted his empty coffee mug around and around. "I was hoping you'd dress up as Santa Claus, Bob," he mumbled.

Neil, Emily, and Carole all laughed.

"Santa Claus! Me?" Bob shook his head. "You *are* joking?"

"No. You'd be perfect. You've got a real way with dogs," the pastor insisted.

"Well, maybe . . . but what about the kids?" asked Bob.

Gavin smiled. "Oh, I'm sure they'll be as good as gold. Will you do it?"

"I don't know . . ." Bob began, making a face.

"Oh, go on, Dad," cried Emily. "You'd be perfect."

"You'd look great in that red suit." Neil chuckled. "You might have to dye your beard, though."

Sarah came into the kitchen carrying her hamster, Fudge, in her cupped hands. She was frowning. "Shhh," she said crossly. "I'm trying to teach Fudge to dance. He wants to be a ballerina, like me." Sarah thought her hamster was the smartest creature in the world.

Neil started to laugh, then quickly changed it to a cough as Sarah turned a furious face toward him. "How's he doing, Squirt?" he asked.

"He was doing really well until you all started laughing and mixed him up," huffed Sarah. "What's so funny, anyway?"

"Dad's going to dress up as Santa and give out presents to dogs and children," Emily explained.

"Why can't the real Santa Claus do it?" asked Sarah.

"He's too busy," said Gavin. "But he's happy that your dad is going to stand in for him." The pastor turned to Bob. "So will you do it?"

"Of course he will," Carole said quickly. "And he'll enjoy every minute of it."

"There's your answer, then," said Bob with a grin. "If Carole says I'll do it, then I'll do it."

"Excellent." Gavin smiled at him. "I've got a big bag of presents in the trunk of my car. I was wondering whether you and Emily might be able to wrap them for me, Neil."

"We'd love to," Emily said eagerly.

"I'll help you bring them in," offered Neil.

The pastor stood up. "Thanks for the coffee, Carole. And thanks for agreeing to stand in for Santa, Bob," he said with a wink. He called to Jet, and the black Labrador stood up and stretched.

"Let us know as soon as there's any news about the baby," said Carole.

"I will. See you soon."

The pastor followed Neil outside. It was still snowing. Large white flakes drifted down thickly from the heavy gray sky. The tracks Neil and Emily had left when they came in from the rescue center were already half filled with snow. Neil tilted his head back so the snow settled onto his face. A few flakes drifted into his open mouth and he let them melt on his tongue.

While Gavin unlocked the trunk of his car, Neil watched Jake and Jet. The two dogs slid along the ground on their tummies, pushing the snow into heaps with their noses and front paws. Then they rolled over, barking excitedly, and leaped up again, sending snow flying up in wild flurries.

Neil groaned. "Typical! Now Jake will have to be dried off again."

Gavin lifted a black garbage bag out of his trunk. "Here you are, Neil. Thanks for agreeing to wrap them." He opened the car door and Jet darted across to him and jumped inside. The Labrador scrambled over the front seat and flopped down on a rug in the back. "Bye, Neil," Gavin called as he started the engine. "Good luck with those puppies. I hope you manage to find homes for all of them."

"Thanks! I'm sure we will," Neil said cheerfully. But he didn't feel quite so sure. If they were going to find homes for Holly and her brothers and sister before Christmas, they'd need all the luck they could get.

# CHAPTER FOUR

"I wish Gavin had bought presents that were easier to wrap," Emily said, pulling a rubber bone out of the plastic bag on the floor. "Some of these things are really tough."

"If you think that's difficult, try one of these," said Neil, waving a pyramid-shaped puzzle at her and making the balls inside it rattle. They were sitting at the kitchen table, wrapping presents for Santaland. Jake lay stretched out on his side in front of the stove, basking in the heat.

"Hey, why don't we phone Jake Fielding about the puppies?" Emily suggested suddenly. Jake was the young reporter for the *Compton News*, and he'd helped the Parkers out before when they'd needed publicity for their rescue dogs. "That article he did about them in the paper when they were first found was excellent. I'm sure he'd do another one about them needing homes — and even take their pictures. I bet lots of people would want to adopt them."

"Great idea, Em!" said Neil. "Let's call him right away. And we could make posters and put them up around Compton."

"Yes. We should put an ad on the King Street Kennels' web site too."

Neil finished wrapping the pyramid puzzle, then got a garbage bag and held it open by the edge of the table. "Slide the wrapped presents in here, then we'll ask Mom if we can use the office computer," he said to Emily.

They hurried into the office and found Carole hard at work on the computer.

"Oh, we were going to make some posters advertising the puppies," Neil explained, looking disappointed. "I suppose we can come back later if you're busy."

Carole shook her head and sighed. "I've had enough of office work for now — I'm exhausted. The computer's all yours."

It didn't take long to make the posters. "They're nice and bright," Emily said proudly as she took the first one out of the printer. She read it aloud: *"Wanted: good homes for gorgeous Labrador retriever puppies. Apply to King Street Kennels, Compton."* Underneath this heading was a photo of the puppies that they'd scanned into the computer. Neil had taken it the day before the puppies were moved from the Parkers' kitchen to the rescue center. They were all sitting on the rug, gazing appealingly at the camera.

Neil phoned Jake Fielding while the posters were printing, and the reporter promised to come over the next day to take the puppies' photo. He said he could probably get the story in that week's issue of the *Compton News*.

"Lots of people will see them in the paper," said Emily when Neil hung up and told her the good news. "I bet we'll get hundreds of people calling about them."

Neil laughed. "We don't need hundreds. Only three. . . . Or four," he added, "if Alex doesn't change her mind about Holly."

"Do you think she will?" Emily asked.

Neil shrugged. "I hope so. Anyway, let's not worry about Alex now. We need to update the King Street Kennels web site." He logged on to the Internet, then added the puppies' descriptions and photo to the web site. "There," he said. "I just hope lots of people read it."

Neil and Emily put the posters into a plastic bag to keep them dry, then set off for Compton with Jake. It had stopped snowing, but there was no sign of a thaw. They walked quickly, their footsteps muffled by the deep snow that covered the sidewalk. "I hope this weather lasts," said Neil as they turned onto the main street. "A white Christmas would be the best!"

Strings of colored lights hung across the main street and most of the shops had a decorated tree in the window.

They reached the supermarket, and Emily took a poster inside. When she came out again, an assistant was already taping it up in the window. "Wow! It looks great!" Neil hollered. "People will spot it a mile away."

"No one will be able to resist having a puppy when they see that photo," said Emily.

They continued down the street, taking posters into the vegetable market and the shoe store. Neil glanced back at them as he walked toward the bakery. "There are already people looking — oof!" He gasped suddenly as he collided with someone and stumbled backward.

Jake darted over and jumped at him. He seemed to think Neil was playing a game. "Get off, you silly dog," Neil said. He gently pushed Jake down and saw Alex standing beside him, holding a loaf of bread and grinning.

"Are you all right?" she asked.

"Fine. Was it you I bumped into?"

"Yes. But it's OK. You've only dented my bread a little." Alex laughed, bending down to pet Jake. "Your

dog's nice," she said, rubbing his head. "What's his name?"

"This is Jake," Emily said.

Neil watched her making a fuss over the Border collie. It was obvious that she loved dogs, and he wished that he could persuade her to take Holly. The two of them would be good for each other.

"We've made some posters advertising the puppies," said Neil. "Do you want to give us a hand with them? We're trying to persuade businesses to put them up." *Maybe helping to find homes for the puppies will make Alex realize that she does want Holly, after all,* he thought.

Alex looked doubtful. "I don't think . . ." she began hesitantly.

"Oh, come on," Neil pleaded, holding out a poster to her. "We could really use some help, couldn't we, Em?"

Emily looked puzzled but she nodded anyway.

"All right, then." Alex took a poster. "Aren't they gorgeous?" she said, looking at the picture. "I should think everyone will —" She broke off and bit her lip, but Neil was certain she'd been about to say that everyone would want to adopt one.

As soon as Alex took the poster into the bakery, Emily turned to Neil.

"Why were you so desperate for Alex to help?" she asked. "I mean, it's not as if we can't manage."

"I thought she'd be more likely to take Holly if she was involved in finding homes for the other puppies," he explained.

"Ah . . . nice idea," Emily said approvingly.

Alex reappeared a minute later, smiling broadly. "They're going to put it up."

"Excellent!" said Neil. He handed Alex another poster. "Do you want to try the candy store next?"

They continued through the center of Compton until they ran out of posters.

"My grandpa used to breed Shelties," Alex said as they turned to walk home. "He goes to lots of dog shows. If you print out some more posters, I'll ask him to put them up in Manchester — if you want."

"That would be great!" Emily said. "The more

people who hear about the puppies, the more chances we've got of finding homes for all of them."

Alex looked wistful for a moment. "Are they all good-natured?" she asked.

"Oh, yes," Emily said. "They've all got their own personalities. Santa's very sweet — he's the little black one. Candy, the golden one, is inquisitive, Cracker's really playful, but Holly's the friendliest."

"Why don't you come and visit Holly at the rescue center?" Neil suggested. "I'm sure she'd be glad to see you. And you could meet her brothers and sister, too."

Alex shook her head unhappily. "No, thanks."

"I expect Holly will be feeling pretty lonely at the moment," Neil went on. "She lived with your mom and dad for four days, so she's used to having people around her. She could definitely use some company." He didn't tell her that he was constantly popping into the rescue center with Emily and Sarah to see the puppies. After spending so many weeks hand-raising them in their kitchen, they all wanted to see as much of the puppies as possible.

Alex shook her head again, more definitely this time. Her eyes were sad. "*Daisy* was my dog. I don't want another one." There was an awkward silence. Neil realized that persuading Alex to take Holly back wasn't going to be easy.

"Why don't you help us with Santaland at the church, then?" asked Emily, changing the subject.

"We promised the pastor we'd wrap all the presents. We've started, but there's tons more to do."

Alex frowned.

"Oh, come on," Neil said. "We'll never get them done on our own." *Maybe we'll be able to persuade Alex to visit Holly once she's at King Street*, he thought hopefully.

Alex nodded. "All right," she agreed, looking a little less miserable.

"Come by tomorrow morning," said Emily. "And —" She broke off suddenly as somebody called her name.

A blond boy was running toward them, weaving in and out of the shoppers on the sidewalk. "Emily! Hey, Emily!"

"It's Tom Charlton," Emily said. "He's in my class at school."

Tom sped up to them, his face glowing with excitement, and skidded to a halt. "I saw your posters!" he said. "I've just moved to a house with a yard and my mom and dad said I could have a dog. Will you save one of your puppies for me?"

"It's not quite as simple as that," Neil explained. "My parents will want to talk to your mom or dad before they let you have one of the puppies. But I'm sure it will be OK," he added quickly as he saw Tom's face fall. "When do you want to come?"

"How about tomorrow morning?" asked Tom eagerly.

"OK, come over at about half past ten," Neil said.

"You won't let them all go before then, will you?" Tom asked.

"No, of course not," Neil promised.

"I don't know which one I'll choose. They're all gorgeous," Tom said.

"They certainly are," Emily agreed.

"See you tomorrow then," said Tom. He raced away.

"Our poster campaign's working!" Emily cried with delight. "At this rate, *all* the puppies will be gone by Christmas."

Neil turned to speak to Alex, but she wasn't there. "Hey, where's Alex gone?" he asked. He looked along the street and saw her hurrying away with her head down. Neil guessed she was thinking about Daisy. But perhaps she was feeling guilty, too, for rejecting Holly when Tom was obviously so enthusiastic about giving one of the puppies a home. Or maybe she was worried that Tom would choose Holly.

"Poor Alex," said Emily. "She looks so unhappy."

"Holly would know just how to cheer her up," said Neil. "We've got to find a way of making her see it. . . ."

# CHAPTER FIVE

"The phone!" Neil cried, jumping up from the breakfast table the next morning. "Perhaps it's somebody calling about the puppies!"

Bob Parker put out a hand to stop Neil. "I don't want you scaring a potential customer away by begging them to take one of the pups." He laughed as he went out of the room to answer it himself.

Neil sat down again. Jake, who was sitting beside him, watched hopefully as Neil bit into a slice of toast. "You've had your breakfast, Jake." Neil laughed.

The Border collie gave him a doggy grin and thumped the floor with his tail.

"That was Gavin, calling from the hospital," said Bob, reappearing in the kitchen doorway. "The baby's on the way now — more than a week early. Poor

Gavin's worried about Santaland and he asked if we could start decorating it later."

"Of course," Emily cried.

"You bet!" whooped Neil.

"What about you, Sarah?" Carole asked. "Do you want to help decorate Santaland?"

Sarah shook her head. "No. I'm giving Fudge a dancing lesson. And I'm making a Christmas card for the puppies."

Bob drained his mug of coffee. "That hamster must be the best dancer in the world." As he headed toward the back door, there was a knock at the front. Emily hurried to answer it and came back with Alex.

"Oh, I'm sorry," said Alex, looking at the breakfast table. "Have I come too early?"

"Of course not," Neil said, reaching for another slice of toast.

"Neil," Carole laughed. "Haven't you had enough yet?"

Neil shook his head. "Nearly. This is Alex, Mom. She's going to help us wrap the presents for Santaland."

"Hello, Alex. Would you like some breakfast?" Carole asked.

"No, thanks," said Alex. "I just had mine."

"Nobody's phoned about the puppies yet," Neil said, while he and Emily cleared the kitchen table. "I visited them this morning. Holly seemed kind of miserable, but she perked up when she saw me." He watched Alex as he spoke. She definitely looked interested when he mentioned Holly, and Neil was convinced it was a good sign.

They sat around the kitchen table and got to work wrapping presents. Jake watched them curiously for a while, then he flopped down by the stove for a nap.

"Maybe the two of us could sell the tickets at Santaland, Alex," suggested Emily.

Alex smiled. "That'd be great! I might get to meet some people then. It's funny living in Compton and not knowing anyone. I had lots of friends in Manchester."

"I'll introduce you to some of my friends from school, if you like," said Neil. "You're going to be in my class, so you'll get to know them soon, anyway."

"I'd like that," Alex said, cutting off a length of ribbon. "By the way, I phoned my grandpa last night and told him about the puppies. He said I could send him some posters — and he's going to call his friends to see if they know anyone who wants a puppy."

"Cool!" Neil finished wrapping a squeaky dog ball and put the package on the growing pile in the middle of the table. "I'll print out some posters for you today."

Just then, Neil heard a car turning into the driveway. He looked out the window to see who it was. "It's Tom and his dad," he told Emily and Alex. "They're right on time — Tom really must be eager!"

As soon as Neil opened the door, Tom asked anxiously, "You did save a puppy for me, didn't you?"

Neil grinned. "Yes, don't worry." It was good to see somebody so truly enthusiastic about adopting a dog. Neil was already sure Tom would make a good owner.

Tom's eyes lit up. "Great," he said, following Neil across the yard to the rescue center. "I've wanted a dog for ages and ages." He grinned at his dad, a friendly looking man with short red hair. "Now I'm finally going to get one at last."

"Wait for us," Emily called as she and Alex came

out of the house. "We're coming, too!" Emily rushed after them, but Neil saw that Alex hesitated.

"How did you persuade her to come?" Neil whispered when Emily caught up with him.

"I said I needed her to help me feed them." Emily grinned.

"Good one!" said Neil.

Bob came out of Kennel Block One and shook hands with Mr. Charlton. "You're interested in one of our Labrador puppies, I hear," he said warmly.

"That's right," agreed Mr. Charlton.

"Come into the office and we'll discuss the details while Tom's choosing the puppy he likes best. Could you take Tom into the rescue center, Neil?"

"Sure." Neil led the way. Holly and Candy trotted up to the wire mesh around their pen and watched as Neil, Emily, and Tom approached. Santa and Cracker, the two black puppies, were curled up in their basket side by side. Cracker opened an eye sleepily, then lumbered to his feet. Santa yawned lazily as he stood up and stretched.

"They're gorgeous!" Tom cried. He crouched down and pushed his fingers through the wire. The puppies crowded around, their tails wagging with excitement. Alex watched from a distance, her face tense and pale.

"There are two girls and two boys," said Neil. He opened the door of the pen and went inside. Emily and Tom followed. Alex hung back at first, but Emily eventually persuaded her to come in. To Neil's delight, Holly rushed straight to Alex, barking a greeting.

"She remembers you!" Emily said.

Alex nodded, frowning. She tried not to look at the puppy, but Holly was clearly determined to be noticed. She tumbled onto Alex's foot and pawed at her leg, whining.

"Do you want to hold her?" asked Neil.

Alex shook her head, but she crouched down and rumpled Holly's silky ears. The puppy licked the inside of Alex's wrist, her tail lashing from side to side. Alex leaned forward and spoke softly to Holly. Neil couldn't hear what she was saying, but he was pleased to see that Alex's frown had faded.

The other three puppies wouldn't leave Tom alone. They banged one another aside in their determination to get his full attention. Eventually, he sat down and let them climb into his lap. "They're fantastic!" he said, beaming at Neil and Emily. "They're just fantastic!"

He picked up Santa and held him against his chest. "But this one's the best of all. Look at his cute little face." The puppy nuzzled Tom's neck, then stretched up and licked his ear.

Tom laughed. "Hey, that tickles! I'd like this one, please. What's his name?"

"Santa," Emily said.

"That's perfect," said Tom.

Emily picked up the other two puppies, so Tom and Santa could get to know each other better. Holly had curled up against Alex's ankle and fallen asleep. Alex was still petting her. Neil felt frustrated. He wouldn't dream of trying to get Alex to take Holly if he thought she didn't want her, but it was clear that a bond was growing between the two of them.

The outer door of the rescue center opened and Bob and Mr. Charlton came in. "All the paperwork's done," Bob announced. "It looks like you and your family will make very good dog owners, Tom."

Tom grinned and stood up, holding Santa carefully. "I've chosen this one, Dad. He's called Santa. Can we take him home now?"

"I'll get the dog carrier from the car." Mr. Charlton laughed.

Santa was soon safely inside the carrier and Tom headed eagerly for the door, obviously impatient to show Santa his new home.

"Thanks very much," Mr. Charlton said, shaking hands with Bob.

"Merry Christmas!" Tom called as he followed his dad out into the snow, carefully holding the carrier.

When Tom and Santa had gone, Emily and Alex fed the remaining puppies.

Neil got a ball and threw it across the pen. The three puppies dashed after it, barking loudly. Then they raced around and around their pen, chasing the ball, each other, and their own tails until at last they flopped down, worn out from so much exercise. Once again, Holly settled down beside Alex, with her head and front paws on Alex's foot.

"She's really fond of you," Neil pointed out.

Alex looked down sadly at the tiny puppy. "She's lovely," she said, "but I just don't want another dog. It's no use trying to persuade me."

"I felt like that when my dog Sam died," Neil began. He thought back to that terrible day when Sam's weak heart had finally failed, after he'd rescued Jake from drowning. "But —"

"Look, Emily told me about that," Alex interrupted. "And I'm sorry about Sam. But it's not the same. You already had Jake. I didn't have another dog . . ." She broke off, obviously trying to make sense of her feelings. "It wouldn't be fair to Daisy," she said at last. Her eyes filled with tears and she brushed them away. "She was the best dog ever."

Emily put her arm around her. "Daisy wouldn't —"

She didn't get a chance to finish because the door of the rescue center opened and Jake Fielding came in. He was a tall young man who wore his long hair in a ponytail. He had a camera slung around his neck and a tripod under his arm. "Your dad said I'd find you in here," he said. "I've come to take some pictures of these puppies of yours for the paper."

"Hi, Jake," said Neil. "Thanks for coming." He

grinned at him, but inside he was feeling even more frustrated. What a shame Jake had arrived at that moment! Neil was pretty sure he and Emily could have convinced Alex to take Holly if they hadn't been interrupted.

"Can you each hold one of the puppies, please?" Jake said as Neil let him into the pen. He quickly set up his tripod and attached his camera to the top.

Emily picked up Holly and plopped her in Alex's arms. Then she scooped up Candy, leaving Neil to hold Cracker.

"Wow, we must be overfeeding you," joked Neil as he picked him up. "You weigh a ton." The puppy nudged Neil with his nose, then stared at the camera.

"Move in closer together," Jake said, bending over to look through the camera's viewfinder. There was a flash as he took the picture.

Holly whimpered. "It's all right, girl," Alex said soothingly.

"I'll just take a couple more," said Jake. His camera flashed again. "Our readers will be happy to see how healthy they look." He took a final photo, then put his camera back in its case and folded up his tripod. "Thanks very much, you guys. They'll be in this week's paper."

"Let's hope it does the trick," Neil said as he put Cracker in the basket.

He watched Alex put Holly down beside her brother. She stroked Holly's head gently. The chocolate-brown Labrador rolled over and Alex petted her tummy.

Neil looked at Emily and they both shook their heads. When was Alex going to realize that she and Holly were made for each other?

# CHAPTER SIX

"Jet's so well trained," said Neil with admiration as Bob parked the Range Rover outside the church later that afternoon. He watched the pastor's black Labrador nosing around the snowy headstones. "He never goes out of the churchyard, you know, even when the gate's open."

"Does he live here, then?" Alex asked in surprise.

"He's the pastor's dog," Neil explained. "He's got his own dog door so he can come and go as he pleases." He pointed to the back door of the pastor's house, which was just visible through the trees on the far side of the churchyard.

Bob opened the car door. "Come on, everybody! No loafing! There's work to be done."

Jake tried to scramble over into the front seat, but

Neil held him back. "Not that way, Jake." He laughed. "Wait your turn!" He climbed out and Jake dashed after him. Emily and Alex followed with the bag of presents.

As they went into the churchyard, Jet came bounding over. Jake sniffed Jet, then sprang away from him and disappeared behind an old weather-beaten gravestone, barking playfully. Jet stared after him for a moment, as though he was trying to decide whether to play or not. He soon made up his mind and ran after the younger dog.

Neil, Emily, and Alex watched the two dogs darting in and out of a row of yew trees in a lively game of tag. "Jake seems to have cheered Jet up!" Emily laughed. She picked up the bag of presents. "Let's get started on the decorations."

"I'll have to leave it to you, I'm afraid," said Bob. "I've got to do some shopping, but I'll be back later."

"Last-minute Christmas presents, by any chance?" Neil said curiously.

Bob grinned. "Never you mind. Just go and get to work." He left the churchyard, shutting the gate behind him.

Neil led the way through the heavy door of the church entryway, which Gavin always kept unlocked during the day. From there, they went through a side door into the stone church, which was hundreds of years old but felt light and airy inside.

Emily put the bag of presents down by the door, making sure that it was ajar so that Jake could get in and out. They found a stepladder and an artificial Christmas tree leaning against a wall. In the middle of the polished wooden floor was a carved chair, a folding screen, and a stack of cardboard boxes filled with Christmas decorations.

"It looks like Gavin has everything we need right here," said Neil. "If we set the screen up over here, Dad can sit behind it." He carried it to the end of the room and opened it up. "People can go in at one end, visit with Dad, get their present, then come out the other end."

"I'm going to start decorating the Christmas tree," Emily said. "It'll look nice in front of that screen."

"I'll give you a hand," Alex offered eagerly. She rummaged through one of the boxes and pulled out lengths of gold and silver wrapping paper. "Hey! These will look great attached to the screen, Neil. We just need some pushpins. . . ."

By the time Jake came trotting in from the churchyard, the screen and ceiling were draped with glittering wrapping paper and the Christmas tree was transformed into a magical creation of glowing lights, gleaming ornaments, and shimmering tinsel. Neil thought it looked fantastic.

The Border collie stopped in the doorway and stared. The Christmas tree lights were reflected in his dark eyes. "What do you think then, Jake?" Emily asked, giving him a pat.

Jake barked once, as though he approved of what he saw, then he pushed past Emily and thrust his head inquisitively into one of the cardboard boxes. When he emerged, strands of silver tinsel hung from his ears.

Neil laughed. "He didn't want to be outdone by a Christmas tree, did you, Jake?" he said from the stepladder, where he was placing a star on the top of the tree.

"I think he looks sweet." Alex chuckled.

Jake turned his attention to another box. It had higher sides than the first box and he couldn't see into it. Suddenly, he jumped up and rested his front paws on the edge of the box. "Don't do that!" Neil cried. His warning came too late — the box toppled over, spilling its contents over the startled dog.

Jake jumped back. A string of Christmas lights was draped across his back now, and scattered around him there were silver bells, plastic reindeer, and snowmen.

"Here, Jake," Neil called, climbing down from the ladder. Jake trotted across to him, trailing the lights. Laughing, Neil lifted the string of lights off the young dog's back and brushed the tinsel from his ears.

"I wonder where Jet's gone," said Emily.

"I hope he's gone back into the house," Neil said.

"If Jake can cause this much trouble on his own, imagine what two dogs could do!"

Alex stood the box up and began to put the decorations back into it. "We could hang these snowmen and reindeer from the coat hooks," she suggested. "And the lights could go around the door."

"Good idea," Emily said, picking up two of the snowmen and hanging them on hooks. She stood back to admire the effect.

"There's an outlet behind the door," Neil said, "so we'll be able to plug in the lights."

Suddenly, they heard footsteps in the church entry, and Jake darted back outside. "How are you doing?" Bob called.

"Come and see, Dad," said Emily.

"Fantastic," Bob said enthusiastically as he looked

around. "Did you put the presents behind the screen?"

"No, they're still in the entryway," said Emily. "I left them by the door because I thought they'd get in the way while we were decorating."

"But you've brought some of them in here?" Bob persisted.

Neil shook his head. "No. We'll bring them in now. We're going to arrange them around your chair."

Bob looked concerned.

"What's wrong?" Neil asked anxiously.

"Come and see," said Bob grimly, ushering them out of the hall.

The sack containing the presents was still by the door where Emily had left it. But as he got closer, Neil could see it was half empty. "Hey, what's happened? Where did all the presents go?"

"Someone must have taken them," Bob said, puzzled.

"You mean stolen them!" said Neil angrily.

"The thief must have come into the entry while we were working on the decorations," Emily said miserably. "We couldn't have heard the door because I left it open for Jake — and we were all talking, anyway."

"But who'd steal Christmas presents from a church?" asked Alex. "That's a horrible thing to do."

"The presents might not have been stolen," Bob said in a calm voice. "You mustn't jump to conclusions."

Neil looked around. "You don't think the thief is still here, do you?"

"He would have run off when he heard Dad coming," Emily said. "But maybe we can find his footprints in the snow and see which way he's gone."

"It's worth a try," said Neil. He whistled for Jake as he went outside. Emily and Alex were close behind him.

But the path through the churchyard was all trampled. There were several sets of footprints on it, and trying to distinguish one set from another was an impossible task.

"What I don't understand is why the thief only took some of the presents," Alex said thoughtfully. "If he heard your dad coming, surely he could have picked up the whole sack and run off with it."

Neil nodded. Alex was right. "Maybe he's planning to come back for the rest of the presents when we've gone home," he said. "He could be hiding somewhere nearby, keeping an eye on us."

Neil searched the churchyard and started to make his way toward the road to see if he could spot anyone suspicious-looking there. Suddenly, he heard a cough behind him. He whirled around, heart thudding. Gavin was walking toward him. "Sorry, Neil," he said. "I didn't mean to startle you. How are you doing with the decorations?"

Neil told the pastor about the missing presents. Gavin shook his head, perplexed. "It must be a misunderstanding. I'm sure nobody would steal little presents like that."

After he and Neil had looked along the road, they headed back to the church hall, lost in thought.

"Has Neil told you about the missing presents?" Emily asked.

Gavin nodded. "But I'm sure there's a perfectly innocent explanation. Let's have a look at Santaland," he said cheerfully.

Neil led the way back to the hall.

"Oh, you've done a wonderful job," the pastor said, clearly impressed.

"It's all been a waste of time, though," Neil said glumly. "The whole thing will have to be canceled if there aren't enough presents for Santa to give out."

"I'll get some more," Gavin said. "People have been looking forward to this, and I can't cancel it now."

"But you won't make any money for the roof repairs if you have to buy more presents," said Emily.

"I'll be happy to supply dog treats, Gavin," Bob offered.

"Thanks, Bob. That's kind of you. That means I only need to buy presents for the children." Gavin smiled at Emily. "Don't look so worried. We'll still make a little bit of profit, it just won't be as much as I'd hoped."

"I think we should hide the rest of the presents," said Neil, "just in case the thief comes back."

"We could tuck some into the Christmas tree,"

Alex suggested. "If we push them in far enough, they'll be hidden in the branches."

"Good idea. And if we leave the hall door open, we can put some packages behind it." Neil scooped up an armful of presents and put them behind the door. Then he pushed the door back against the wall to hide them, while Emily stuffed what was left under the cushion on Santa's chair.

"I've got some good news," Gavin said when they'd finished.

"Oh, we forgot!" said Emily. "Did Susie have the baby?"

Gavin beamed at all of them. "A boy. Joshua."

"Congratulations, Gavin," Bob cried, slapping him on the back.

"Thanks." Gavin looked at his watch. "I'd better get a move on. I only dropped by to feed Jet and take him for a walk. I want to get back to the hospital as soon as I can."

"We could feed Jet for you, if you want," suggested Neil. "And then we could take him for a long run."

Gavin's smile broadened. "That would be wonderful, Neil. Thanks." He handed Neil his back-door key. "I've got a key to the front door, so drop this one into the mailbox after you've locked up." He hurried away.

"I ought to go, too," Alex said. "My parents will be wondering where I've gone."

"Oh, I'll give you a lift, Alex," said Bob. "You two can walk back after you've taken care of Jet."

"OK," Neil agreed. He whistled for Jake, and he and Emily made their way around the gravestones to Gavin's back door.

"I wonder who did steal the presents," Emily said. "They can't be worth very much."

"Whoever it is will get a shock when he unwraps them," Neil said with a chuckle. "Imagine his face when he finds out he's stolen a bunch of rubber bones and dog biscuits!"

# CHAPTER SEVEN

Alex was at the door of King Street Kennels just after nine o'clock the next morning. "I hope you don't mind . . . I wanted to see the puppies."

Neil was overjoyed. Perhaps, at last, she was ready to admit that she wanted Holly. Not that she looked particularly happy, he thought as he led the way through the house to the back door.

"I want to say good-bye to them," explained Alex sadly. "I expect they'll all be gone soon and my mom said I'd be upset if I hadn't seen Holly for one last time. . . . She's probably right."

Neil felt a rush of sympathy for Alex as he put on his coat and boots. "Come on then," he said gently, leading the way across the snowy yard.

The puppies were lying in a contented heap in

their basket fast asleep when Neil and Alex went into the rescue center. "They're so sweet," Alex said wistfully, watching them through the wire fence.

At the sound of Alex's voice, Holly opened her eyes. She jumped out of the basket and raced across to the fence. "She's pleased to see you," said Neil. He paused, then added, "She does seem to respond to you more than anyone else, you know." Just seeing the two of them together made Neil feel hopeful again. If anyone could persuade Alex to take Holly, it was the puppy herself.

Holly pressed against the wire, whining a greeting. Alex pushed her fingers through and stroked

Holly's silky chest. The Labrador pup licked her hand, then tried to climb up the inside of the fence toward Alex's face, her tail wagging vigorously.

Neil let Alex into the pen, then started to prepare the puppies' food. Alex sat on the floor with Holly curled up in her lap. She was stroking the pup's chocolate-brown fur while Holly gazed up at her.

Neil took the food into the pen and Cracker and Candy woke up. They leaped joyfully out of their basket and raced across to the bowl, yapping with excitement. Holly stood up on Alex's lap. She hesitated for a moment, watching Alex intently. "Go and get your breakfast, girl," Alex said, giving her a gentle push.

Holly jumped down and ran to the bowl, nudging her way in between her brother and sister.

"They're great, aren't they?" said Neil.

Alex smiled. "Especially Holly. She seems so friendly and intelligent. I bet she'd be really easy to train and —" She broke off and a look of dismay flashed across her face.

Neil groaned inwardly. One moment he was sure Alex would take Holly, the next he was sure she wouldn't. "Having another dog wouldn't make you forget Daisy," he said at last.

Alex stood up. "No," she said firmly. "I don't want another dog. It would be . . . disloyal." She headed for the door of the pen but, before she reached it, the outer door of the rescue center opened and Bob showed a middle-aged couple in. "Ah, Neil. There you are," he said. "Mr. and Mrs. Grant have come to choose a puppy. They'd like a female one."

Alex froze. Then she turned and looked back at Holly, her face stiff with anxiety.

"Aren't they adorable?" said Mrs. Grant.

Neil let them into the pen and Mrs. Grant bent down and called to the puppies. They looked up from their bowl, hesitated, then continued to eat. "They'll probably come to you as soon as they've finished eating," Neil told the Grants. "The golden one and the brown one are both girls."

He turned to Alex. "Look, why don't you take Holly?" he whispered urgently. "If you don't, someone else will."

"I don't want her." Alex spoke fiercely but her eyes were sad.

"The brown one's gorgeous," said Mr. Grant as Holly trotted away from the bowl. He picked her up. "She looks sturdy and intelligent."

Mrs. Grant picked up Candy. "This one's lovely, too," she said, laughing as the pup licked her ear. She turned to her husband. "I can't decide. You pick."

"We'll have this chocolate one, then," Mr. Grant said.

Alex went pale.

"Actually," said Neil quickly, "that one's already promised to someone. Sorry, I should have made that clear," he mumbled awkwardly. "But the golden puppy — Candy — is just as sweet, don't you think?"

The Grants looked puzzled. "All right," Mr. Grant said, putting Holly down gently and giving her a pat. "We'll take Candy instead. The color's not important, and they both seem friendly."

"Our daughter's gone away to college," Mrs. Grant explained as Neil showed them out of the rescue center. Candy was snuggled in her arms, and Neil was pleased to see how quickly the puppy had taken to her new owner. "We've been lonely without her, and we thought a dog would help to fill the gap."

"We're going to bring her to your dad's obedience classes," added Mr. Grant as they set off across the yard to the office to sign the forms.

"I'll see you there, then," Neil called after them. He went back into the rescue center. Alex was holding Holly in her arms. As Neil came near, he saw that she was close to crying.

"Who's Holly promised to?" Alex asked in a wobbly voice.

"You, if you want her," said Neil gently. "But we really can't keep her forever, Alex. The next time somebody wants her, we'll have to let her go." He picked up Cracker and scratched his ears.

Alex nodded and blinked her tears away. "I know and I don't want her," she said decisively. "I really don't." She put Holly down in the basket and went out of the pen. "And anyway, my grandpa phoned last night. He thinks he knows someone who might like one of them."

"That's great," said Neil. He put Cracker down beside his water bowl and followed Alex out, shaking his head in confusion.

"I don't believe it — the thief has been here again!" Emily cried. "I left four presents under this cushion and now there are only two." Neil, Emily, and Alex had decided to go back to the church to check on the presents and to see if they could find any clues to the identity of the thief.

Alex ran to the Christmas tree. "One's been taken from here as well," she said, dismayed.

"But how on earth did the thief know where to look?" Neil asked, mystified. He looked behind the door, and sure enough, one of the presents he'd left there had vanished as well.

They exchanged puzzled looks. "Why did he only take some of the presents again?" Emily asked.

"And this is weird, too," Neil said. "It hasn't snowed since last night, but I noticed that there's only one set of footprints leading to and from the church. They must be Gavin's, so where are the thief's?"

Emily and Alex followed him to the church door. Neil pointed to the tracks. "See?" he said. "Those footprints lead from the house to the church and back again. And there are Jet's paw prints beside them — although he was obviously running around a bit because his tracks go all over the place."

"So the thief must have come back before last night's snowfall," Alex said.

Neil nodded. "It looks like it. Let's go and ask Gavin if he noticed anything yesterday when he locked up the church for the night."

They hurried to the house and rang the bell. "Hello, everybody," said Gavin as he opened the door for them. "I was just about to go to the hospital to pick up Susie and Joshua. What can I do for you?"

"Some more presents have disappeared from the church," Neil said.

Gavin frowned. "You're joking!" he said. "Even after you'd hidden them? I know they were all there last night when I locked up because I checked them."

Neil looked thoughtful. "So that means they must have been taken during the night."

"But the church was locked all night," said Gavin. "I don't understand how anyone could have gotten in. . . . Look, I've really got to go now. I'll have to leave you to solve the mystery."

Neil, Emily, Alex, and Jake made their way back to the church and examined the door for signs of a break-in. But both the door and the lock were undamaged, the windows couldn't be opened, and none of the panes of glass had been broken.

"He must have a key, then," Neil said. "It's the only explanation."

"I know! Why don't we put a bag stuffed with paper by the door, to see if we can lure him into coming back today," suggested Alex.

"Good idea," said Neil, leading the way back to the church. He rummaged in the boxes of decorations. "This will do," he said, pulling out some sheets of dog-eared Christmas wrapping paper.

They filled the bag with balls of paper and Neil set it in the doorway. "Let's hide and keep watch for a while. The thief must have come by at about this time yesterday, so it's worth a try," he said. He patted Jake. "How about it, boy? Do you want to do a little doggy detective work?"

Jake gave an eager bark and jumped up, putting his front paws on Neil's chest.

"Good for you." Neil laughed.

"Where shall we hide?" asked Emily.

They looked around. "Somewhere near the door," Neil said, "so we can see people coming and going." He pointed to a huge, ancient gravestone covered in moss. "That one looks big enough to hide us all."

As they crouched down behind it, Jet trotted up. "Hello, boy," Emily said. "Have you come to help?"

Jet wagged his tail and squeezed in between Emily and Alex while Jake pressed against Neil. "At least we've got the dogs to keep us warm," Neil said in a low voice. "It's freezing out here." Although he was wearing gloves, his fingers were already numb from the cold, and he rubbed his hands together vigorously.

"As long as they don't make a noise and give us away," said Alex.

They settled down to watch. Out on the road a truck drove past, puffing out a cloud of dirty exhaust fumes. Birds huddled together on the church roof and they saw an occasional shopper pass by, laden down with bulging bags. But nobody came into the churchyard.

Jake and Jet grew impatient with the long wait and wandered off to play. Neil could see them now and then, darting in and out among the headstones.

Time passed slowly. Gray clouds were beginning to build up overhead. "I think it's going to snow again," Alex said at last.

They all stared at the sky. "Let's give up and go home," said Emily, her teeth chattering. "I'm frozen." She came out from behind the gravestone and Alex followed her, looking relieved.

Neil stood up and stretched his cramped legs. "Yeah, I guess you're right. It doesn't look as though he's coming back today," he admitted reluctantly. He was frustrated that they hadn't been able to solve the mystery. Keeping watch at night seemed like a better bet, though. Surely the thief was more likely to come back then — when he would be pretty sure that there would be no one around to see what he was up to. . . .

"I'm coming back tonight," said Neil decisively.

"What, by yourself?" asked Alex.

Neil nodded.

"I'll come with you," Emily offered.

"There's no point in both of us getting frozen. And there's no point in Mom and Dad getting mad at both of us if they find out, either."

"But it'll be dark. And you'll be in a graveyard," Alex persisted.

"So?" Neil shrugged. "I've got to get to the bottom of this."

"Won't you be scared?" asked Alex.

"I'll have Jake with me," Neil pointed out. He

whistled and the Border collie obediently came running up to him.

"Come on," Emily said impatiently. "If we don't go home soon, I'm going to turn into an icicle."

Snow began to fall, driven across the churchyard by an icy wind. "You won't come back tonight if it's snowing like this, will you?" Alex asked, shivering.

"Of course I will," said Neil. He wouldn't let a little bad weather get in his way. He was determined to catch the thief, and nothing was going to stop him.

# CHAPTER EIGHT

Neil's alarm rang at midnight. He jumped up, startled by its loudness, then reached out and switched it off. The house felt cold as he climbed out of bed, and he got ready quickly, shivering uncontrollably.

When he was dressed, Neil picked up his flashlight, opened his bedroom door a crack, and listened. The house was silent. Neil tiptoed along the landing and down the stairs.

Jake was asleep in the kitchen. He looked up in surprise when Neil crept in, but he stood up and trotted to greet him all the same. "Good boy, Jake," Neil said, clipping on his leash. He unlocked the back door and he and Jake slipped outside.

It had been snowing all afternoon and the snow in the yard behind the house was almost knee deep.

Neil frowned, knowing that the tracks he and Jake left would give him away unless it snowed again after he got home. Still, he was determined to go ahead with his plan. He headed out with his wool hat pulled down over his ears and his collar turned up, but the icy wind still cut right through him.

Once he reached the churchyard, he hesitated. During the day it had been easy to say that he wouldn't be scared, but now the moon cast an eerie glow across the snow-covered headstones and he began to feel uneasy. He looked around anxiously. Everything was still. Tentatively, he pushed the gate open and went inside.

Neil held Jake's collar and made his way between the graves, glad to have the Border collie's company. He reached the huge gravestone near the church door, brushed away the snow from behind it and sat down to wait. The gravestone offered some protection from the wind and, with Jake pressed up against him, Neil began to warm up a little.

"Let's hope he comes soon, Jake," he whispered. Jake whined and twisted his head so he could lick Neil's cheek.

The long, silent night wore on, but nobody came. At one point, Neil heard two men talking softly as they walked along the road toward the church. He stiffened and waited expectantly, but they passed by.

Neil began to feel sleepy. He shifted his position, knowing it would be dangerous to fall asleep in the cold, but it was hard to stay awake with nothing to do but stare into the darkness. And it seemed to be getting darker. Neil glanced up at the sky. Most of the stars had been blotted out by clouds, and the moon was half covered, too. He groaned inwardly. Surely it wasn't going to snow again. Still, at least his tracks would be covered up if it did. . . .

Sure enough, snow began falling. Neil switched on his flashlight, hunching over it to shield the light from anyone who might be watching, and looked at his watch. It was ten past two. He switched the flashlight off again and willed the thief to come. "We'll give him another fifteen minutes, Jake," he whispered. "Then we'll go home."

Jake leaped up.

"What is it, boy?" Neil reached for Jake's collar but, before he could grab it, the young dog rushed away around the side of the church.

"Jake!" Neil hissed. "Come back!" He got up, knowing he had to find Jake. If he *had* heard the thief, the Border collie could be in danger. Quickly switching on his flashlight, Neil charged after him.

The churchyard was shadowy. Neil whirled his flashlight around, desperately looking for Jake, but the snow was falling fast now and the flakes got into his eyes. He brushed them away impatiently as he ran between the gravestones, swinging the flashlight from left to right. "Jake, where are you?" he called softly.

Suddenly, Neil saw a dark shape dart behind a gravestone on the far side of the churchyard. He dashed toward it. "Jake," he hissed. "Here, boy."

Then two shapes shot out of the shadows. Neil jumped with fright, his heart hammering. But soon he relaxed as he swung the flashlight beam around and saw that it was Jake and Jet. Jake was all right! He must have heard Jet coming out through his dog door and run off to play!

The dogs ran up to Neil, barking a greeting. "You gave me a scare," he scolded, patting each of them in turn. Then he clipped on Jake's leash. "Come on, you two. There's no point in hanging around here any longer. If the thief was lurking nearby, he'll have run a mile after that performance."

He led Jake to Gavin's back door and Jet trotted along behind. Neil held the dog flap open. "In you go, Jet. It's too cold for you to be out here in the middle of the night."

The black Labrador gave a last nudge to Jake, then pushed through the dog door. Neil let it close behind him and headed home with Jake.

Neil slept late the next morning. When he got downstairs, Carole was clearing the breakfast table. "Morning, sleepyhead," she said.

"Morning," said Neil. She didn't look angry, he thought with relief, so she obviously didn't know about his midnight outing yet. He pushed a slice of bread into the toaster.

"Would you like some hot chocolate?" Carole asked.

"Yes, please," Neil said, yawning.

"Guess what?" Emily called, running into the kitchen. "Someone's coming from Manchester to see the puppies. A boy named Michael Todd and his mom. They know Alex's grandpa."

"Oh . . . that's good, I suppose," Neil said hesitantly. He knew he should be pleased at the thought of finding a home for another of the puppies, but he was worried, too. What if they chose Holly? If they did, he knew Alex would be devastated. And if they chose Cracker and Alex still refused to have Holly, then the puppy would be alone in the rescue center for Christmas.

"Aren't you pleased?" Emily asked.

"I am, really," Neil began. "It's just —"

"I know," interrupted Emily. "You think it would be best if Holly went to Alex. But it doesn't look like she'll change her mind, and time's running out."

Before Neil could reply, Sarah came rushing into the kitchen, wearing a tinsel crown on her head. "Dad's going to buy the Christmas tree later. And we're going to decorate it after dinner. And I'm an angel."

Neil laughed as he spread butter on his toast. "Does that mean you're going to be good?"

"I'm always good," said Sarah indignantly. "Aren't I, Mom?"

"Most of the time," Carole said, setting Neil's mug of hot chocolate down on the counter. "Here you are, Neil. I'll be out in Kennel Block One. Can you let me know when the people from Manchester get here?" She put on her coat and went out.

Neil looked outside, hoping she wouldn't notice the tracks he and Jake left the night before, but the snow in the yard was deeper than ever and he knew they must have been filled in.

Just then, the doorbell rang and Neil ran to answer it.

Alex was on the step. "Hi," she said. "I've come to see how you did last night."

Neil shook his head. "No luck. Jake and I waited

for ages, but no one showed up." As he stood aside to let her in, a car pulled into the driveway.

Alex looked around.

"We're expecting some people from Manchester," Neil explained. "They know your grandpa, and they want one of the puppies." He saw Alex's face cloud over. "Look — I can tell them that Holly's already promised to you, if you want. You've still got time to change your mind —"

"No, thanks," Alex interrupted, looking down at the ground.

"Come on!" said Emily, racing past them. "Oh, hello, Alex. Let's go show the puppies to the Todds."

A woman and a boy of about eight climbed out of the car parked in the courtyard. Neil stopped to talk to them while Alex and Emily went on ahead to the rescue center.

Just then, Carole came out of Kennel Block One. "I thought I heard a car," she said, smiling. "You must be Mrs. Todd. Thanks for coming. Were the roads very bad?"

Mrs. Todd laughed wryly. "They could have been better," she said, "but we're here now. That's the main thing. Michael's been so excited since he found out we were getting another dog."

Michael, a serious-looking boy with glasses and dark, cropped hair, tugged his mother's hand. "Can we see the puppies now, Mom? Please?"

"Of course you can," Carole said and led the way to the rescue center.

Emily and Alex were already inside. Alex was throwing a ball for Holly and the puppy was scampering after it. Cracker was lying in the basket, lazily watching his sister's antics.

Neil opened the pen and he and Michael went inside. Alex watched Michael anxiously as he looked from Holly to Cracker and back again. "They're great, aren't they?" he said. Holly charged toward him with the ball in her mouth, and he stooped down to pet her. Cracker got to his feet slowly and padded over to meet the newcomer, too.

"Shep, my last puppy, was run over," Michael said sadly, glancing at Alex and Emily. "It was terrible. I thought I'd never want another dog but I've changed my mind now. I still miss Shep, but it's awful not having a dog at home." He grinned at the girls. "Which one do you want?"

Emily glanced at Alex. Neil knew that she was hoping Alex would tell him she'd chosen Holly — but Alex didn't say anything.

"We're not here to choose a puppy," Emily said at last. "I live here — and Alex is my friend."

Carole and Mrs. Todd came toward the pen, talking. "Of course, Michael was devastated when Shep was run over," Mrs. Todd was saying. "But there are so many dogs in need of good homes that it seems a shame not to have another one. Michael soon got used to the idea."

"I agree," Carole said. "Committed dog owners are hard to find."

Neil watched Alex's face. She looked guilty and confused. Maybe seeing Michael choose a new puppy after losing his old dog would finally help her feel OK about adopting Holly.

"Have you chosen, Michael?" Mrs. Todd asked.

Michael reached out a hand to both puppies. Cracker rolled over to have his tummy stroked. Holly darted to Alex, dropped the ball, and tugged at her shoelace. "I think this black one has chosen me," Michael said, grinning. He picked up the puppy and held him against his chest. "He's great, isn't he, Mom?"

"He certainly is," agreed Mrs. Todd.

Neil waited until the Todds and Carole had gone out of the rescue center to fill out the paperwork, then he turned to Alex. "I think Holly has chosen you, Alex."

Alex blushed. "I shouldn't have come," she said sadly. "It's not fair to Holly. She might want to live with me, but I can't have her." She opened the door of the pen and started to walk away. "I won't come again. And I hope you hurry up and find somebody to take her," she called.

Emily raced after her. Neil picked Holly up. He didn't want the little puppy to be alone just yet. It would probably take her a while to adjust to life without any brothers or sisters. "That's it, then, girl," he said sadly. "I've done my best, but Alex just doesn't see that the two of you belong together."

Holly's eyes began to close. Gently, Neil laid her in her basket. "We'll just have to find someone else to love you," he said with a sigh.

# CHAPTER NINE

"Enjoy yourself, Santa Claus," Carole called from the door as Bob unlocked the Range Rover. "I hope that Santaland's a success." Neil, Emily, Sarah, and Jake piled into the back and Alex got into the front seat.

"Enjoy myself? There's not much chance of that!" Bob replied with a grin. "I mean, think of that beard!"

"You'll be fine," Carole assured him.

"Are you sure you don't want to come, Mom?" asked Emily.

Carole shook her head. "There's too much to do here. Bev and Kate have been working like crazy to prepare for our Christmas boarders, and one of us ought to be around to give them a hand."

Bob started the engine and carefully steered the

Range Rover through the snow to the end of the driveway. "The roads don't look too bad," he said as he turned toward Compton. "I thought we'd have to walk to the church when I got up this morning — it must have been snowing most of the night."

"It's a shame the real Santa Claus couldn't come," sighed Sarah.

"He's too busy getting ready for tomorrow night," Neil explained. "He's probably starting to load the sleigh already."

Sarah giggled with excitement. "I wish Christmas would hurry up. I can't wait to see what Santa brings me." She suddenly became serious. "I won't tell anybody you're not the real Santa Claus, Dad," she promised.

"Good for you. We don't want people to be disappointed," said Bob as he pulled up outside the church. "Come on, everyone. Let's get a move on. I've still got to get changed."

They hurried to the pastor's house and rang the bell. Gavin came to the door. "Hello, Bob. Thanks for coming so early," he said gratefully. He showed Bob into his study, where the Santa suit was hanging, and left him to change. "Why don't the rest of you come into the warm kitchen?"

Jet was lying by the stove. He lifted his head and looked at them as they came in, then flopped down again. "He doesn't look too lively," Neil said, crouching down to pat him.

Gavin frowned. "He's been a bit low lately."

Sarah went to pet the black Labrador. "He's really excited about seeing Santa," she said. Then she added in a whisper, "He doesn't know it's only Dad dressed up." Jake trotted over to her and lay down beside Jet with his head resting on the older dog's back.

"Oh, I nearly forgot," said Neil suddenly. "We've brought a few posters with us advertising the last of our Labrador puppies. Would you mind if we put them up in the church?"

"Not at all," Gavin said.

Susie, Gavin's wife, came into the kitchen. "I thought I heard voices," she said, smiling at everyone.

"Hello," said Emily. "How's Joshua?"

"He's fine — he's asleep upstairs. Would you all like to see him?"

"Oh, yes, please!" Emily said enthusiastically.

Neil couldn't see why anyone would get so excited about seeing a new baby. If Gavin and Susie had a new puppy, that would be different. . . .

As they went out of the kitchen, Jake got up to follow them. "You stay here, Jake," Neil commanded.

"It's all right," said Susie. "Jake can come, too, if he likes. Joshua has to get used to dogs."

"Come on then, Jake," Neil said. "But be quiet. You'll be in trouble if you wake the baby."

Susie led the way upstairs. "He's in here," she said

softly. A double bed occupied most of the floor space, but there was a wicker crib standing beside it. “Go in and have a look at him,” said Susie. “I’m just going to run myself a bath.”

They crept into the room and gathered around the crib. The baby was fast asleep, his downy blond hair standing up in wisps and his tiny hands clutching his quilt. “Isn’t he sweet?” Alex whispered.

“I wish we could take him home,” said Sarah.

Suddenly, Neil heard a rustling and crunching sound behind him. Leaving the girls to admire Joshua, he turned quickly, worried that Jake was up to mischief. The Border collie was lying halfway under Gavin and Susie's bed. He seemed to be chewing on something.

"What have you got there, Jake?" Neil asked. He bent down to see, then drew back in astonishment. Jake was chewing a rubber bone wrapped in paper. Neil recognized it. It was one of the presents from the church.

"Where did you get that? Come out of there." As Jake crawled out from under the bed, Neil saw that there were more presents there. Hardly able to believe his eyes, he bent down to have a better look. There was no doubt about it. The missing presents were piled under the pastor's bed!

Neil took the rubber bone away from Jake, then sat back on his heels to think. Surely Gavin hadn't stolen the presents himself. But what other explanation could there be? The last place a thief would think to hide them would be in the pastor's house.

He looked around to see if anyone else had noticed, but Emily, Sarah, and Alex were still looking at the baby.

Just then, Jet came into the bedroom. To Neil's surprise, he was carrying one of the presents from the church in his mouth. He squirmed under the bed, deposited the present on the pile, and wriggled out again. Then he lay down beside Neil, looking rather pleased with himself.

"Jet's the thief!" Neil cried.

"What?" Emily said, whirling around in astonishment. "He can't be!"

"He is." Neil showed her the stack of presents. "He just brought one in and added it to the pile."

"The baby's waking up," Alex said.

Neil's hand flew to his mouth. "I'd forgotten all about him."

Joshua began to cry, and Susie rushed into the bedroom and picked him up.

"Sorry," Neil apologized. "It was my fault. I just discovered what happened to your missing presents and I forgot to be quiet."

"What do you mean?" asked Gavin, coming into the room.

Neil pointed to the bed. "They're here — Jake found them. It looks like Jet's been taking them all along."

Gavin bent down and peeked under the bed. He ruffled Jet's fur. "What on earth have you been up to, Jet?" He pulled out a few of the presents. "They look all right," he said. "I should be able to take the second batch I bought back to the store and get a refund."

"The dogs will get more exciting presents, too, instead of just dog treats," Neil said.

"And the church will make some money for the roof repairs," said Emily.

Gavin smiled. "Yes, it will. And it's all thanks to you, Neil, and to Jake."

"How did Jet take the presents during the night, though?" asked Alex. "The church is closed then."

Gavin looked thoughtful. "Well, he came with me when I went to lock up. I was there for a while, sorting a few things out, so I guess he could have taken them then. He must have gone back and forth from the church to the house to steal all those presents, though — and I didn't even notice."

"We saw that he'd left lots of tracks in the snow," Emily said.

"And being a dog, he'd be able to sniff the presents out," Neil added, "even after we'd hidden them. Does he usually take things?"

Gavin shook his head. "Not that I know of."

"So why has he suddenly started it now?" asked Neil, thinking out loud.

"He's been kind of moody and depressed lately," Gavin said. "And I've been feeling bad because I haven't had time to walk him much."

"He's probably been stealing to get your attention then," Neil said knowledgeably. "He must feel a little left out. Dogs often feel like that when there's a new baby in the family."

"Oh, poor Jet!" cried Susie. She called him, and the Labrador trotted eagerly to her. "We still love you, boy," she said, rubbing the side of his head with her free hand. The big dog's tail wagged happily.

"Let's get the presents out," Gavin said, lying down and reaching under the bed.

Suddenly, they heard a voice from downstairs. "Ho-ho-ho!"

"It's Santa Claus!" cried Sarah.

"It's Dad." Neil laughed. They each carried an armful of presents downstairs. Bob was standing in the hall, dressed in his Santa outfit. His face was almost hidden by a white beard that was even bushier than his real one. "How do I look?" he asked.

Jake sat at Bob's feet and gazed up at him with his head to one side, as though he couldn't imagine why Bob was dressed in such strange clothes. Neil burst out laughing.

"It's not that bad, is it?" Bob asked.

"Worse!" Neil grinned. He put the presents down on the hall table. "I wouldn't want to be seen in an outfit like that."

"It wouldn't fit you, anyway," Sarah said, taking Bob's hand protectively and scowling at Neil.

"But the elf suit would," said Bob. He turned to Gavin. "That elf suit you've got hanging in your study looks exactly the right size for Neil."

Neil stared at his dad in horror. "No way!" he said. "I'm not dressing up as an elf for anybody."

"But Gavin got it out just for you," Bob persisted, with a twinkle in his eye.

Neil shook his head firmly. "Absolutely not!"

Emily, Alex, and Sarah laughed. "Make him wear it, Dad," begged Emily. "Then we can take a picture of him and hang it up at home for everyone to see."

Alex glanced at her watch. "Santaland's supposed to be opening in a few minutes," she reminded them. "Do you think we ought to get over to the church?"

They went out into the snow, with Jake and Jet bounding ahead of them. A line of people and dogs were waiting outside. They cheered when they saw Santa Claus. Neil recognized most of them. He stopped to speak to Doctor Harvey and to make a fuss over his two dogs, Finn and Sandy. Mr. Hamley, Neil's principal, was in line, too, with Dotty, his wayward Dalmatian. Neil wished he had time to greet all of the dogs, but Gavin was obviously in a hurry to open Santaland.

Bob went into the church and sat on the tinsel-covered chair behind the screen. Emily arranged the presents on either side of him — one pile for children and another for dogs — while Alex switched on the Christmas lights and Neil hung up the posters with Holly's picture on them. "Let's hope these do the trick," he said to himself.

"Are you ready?" Gavin asked, sticking his head around the door.

"I think so," said Neil. He peeked behind the screen. "Good luck, Dad."

"Thanks," Bob said, tugging at his white beard. "This thing is driving me nuts already, and I haven't even started yet." He chuckled. "I don't know how I let myself get talked into this."

Emily and Alex stood at the edge of the screen, ready to take the money.

"Ladies, gentlemen, children, and dogs," Gavin said from the other side of the door. "I declare this Santaland open." He flung the door wide and people began to pour inside, admiring the Christmas tree and the decorations. A line quickly formed by the screen, and Emily and Alex began to collect the money.

Sarah was working her way around the room, petting all the dogs and saying hello to school friends.

Neil couldn't help smiling as he watched her — she looked ready to burst at having to keep Santa's true identity a secret.

Looking around the room, he could see excitement on lots of faces. *Only two more days to go!* he thought. Then he spotted the poster of Holly and his happiness evaporated. It wouldn't be much of a Christmas for the Labrador puppy unless they could find her a home.

The crowd was finally thinning when Gavin appeared with a tray of hot chocolate. "Could you take one of these in to Santa, please, Neil?"

"Sure." Neil went behind the screen and waited until Bob's visitor had finished, then he handed him the cup.

"Just what I need!" Bob croaked. "I've said 'Ho-ho-ho' so many times that I've almost lost my voice."

"How's it going, apart from that?" asked Neil.

Bob fiddled with the white beard. "I'm so hot I feel like I've been cooked, and this beard is tickling my nose. But I've patted lots of friendly dogs, seen lots of cheerful faces, and heard about all the things the children of Compton would like for Christmas. I've nearly run out of presents, though. How many people are still waiting to see me?"

"Only four or five," Neil said. "But one of them is Mrs. Jepson. Sugar and Spice are really looking forward to seeing you," he added with a laugh.

"Oh, no! Spare me!"

"I'll leave you to it," said Neil with a grin.

A young couple was looking at one of the posters of Holly when he came out from behind the screen. A red setter was sitting listlessly at their feet, her head drooping and her eyes half closed.

Neil went over and crouched down beside her. He held out a hand to her. "Hello, girl. What's up?"

The dog sniffed him halfheartedly, and he patted her gently.

"Your dog doesn't look too happy," Neil said to its owners. He stood up.

The couple turned. "I know," the woman said anxiously. "Poor Topsy. We have a vet's appointment today, but a friend of ours thinks she might be lonely." She pointed to the poster. "We've been thinking about getting a puppy to keep her company. That one looks perfect."

Neil hesitated before he answered. He was still secretly hoping Alex would change her mind. But he knew they'd run out of time — Holly needed a home now. "I'm the person you need to speak to about the puppy," Neil told the couple eventually. "My name's Neil Parker and I live at King Street Kennels.

Holly's a great little dog — really friendly. Do you want to meet her?"

"Yes, we'll go right over, if that's OK," the man said eagerly. "It'll be nice to have a puppy in the house again at Christmas." Neil gave them directions to the kennels, and they hurried out of the hall with Topsy trailing behind them.

As soon as they had gone, Neil raced over to Emily. "That couple is going over to see Holl —" He broke off quickly as Alex came out from behind the screen.

She stared at him in shock. "Do you mean they're going to adopt her?" she said in a wobbly voice.

"Yes, I'm afraid so," said Neil, looking at his feet.

Alex's eyes filled with tears. "No! We've got to stop them! Holly's *my* dog. I want her to live with *me*."

"But why didn't you say something before?" asked Neil, exasperated. "We gave you so many chances to change your mind! It's too late now."

"I didn't feel like this before." Alex sobbed. "I mean, I liked Holly but it seemed wrong to want another dog — after Daisy."

Emily smiled sadly at Alex. "There'll be other dogs at the rescue center. You can always have one of those."

Alex sobbed harder than ever. "I don't want any other dog. I only want Holly." She grabbed Neil's arm. "We've got to stop those people. We've got to tell them Holly's already got an owner."

Neil shook his head sadly. "I'm sorry, Alex," he

said, "but it's too late. There's nothing we can do now. If they want her, then she's theirs."

Neil stared out of the window of the Range Rover as Bob drove back to King Street Kennels. Compton was ablaze with colored lights but Neil hardly noticed them. He was too upset about what had happened.

Beside him, Alex and Emily sat in miserable silence. Even Sarah was subdued.

As Bob reached the kennels, a car turned out of the driveway. Neil recognized the young couple inside it — the people he'd spoken to at the church. He looked into the car and caught a glimpse of Holly sitting next to the red setter on the back seat.

Alex had seen the puppy, too. "It's Holly!" she cried and burst into tears again.

As Bob parked the car, Carole came out to meet them, smiling. "Holly's gone," she said cheerfully. "Mr. and Mrs. Biggs have taken her. They seem really nice. Apparently their other dog —" She stopped when she saw Alex's miserable face. "What on earth's wrong?" she asked.

"Alex just realized that she wants Holly, after all," explained Emily.

"Oh dear, you poor thing." Carole sighed. "Let's go inside and talk about it." She led Alex into the kitchen.

Neil and Emily followed a few minutes later and

found Alex sitting at the kitchen table with a box of tissues and a glass of soda in front of her. They decided that it was best to leave her with their mom and went on into the living room. The Christmas tree stood in the window, glittering brightly.

"It doesn't feel like Christmas anymore," Emily said gloomily.

"This whole thing is my fault," said Neil, slumping into a chair beside the fire.

"No, it isn't," Emily said. "You tried to get Alex to take Holly. We both did."

"But I told those people how great Holly is, too."

Neil grabbed a cushion and punched it angrily. "Why didn't I say she already had a home? Then Alex could have had her."

Emily sat on the arm of his chair. "Alex insisted she didn't want her," she pointed out. "And we couldn't have kept Holly in the rescue center forever while we waited for Alex to change her mind. Especially not at Christmas."

Sarah came into the room and stood by the Christmas tree, touching the ornaments and setting them swinging so that they twinkled in the firelight. "Why's everybody so grumpy?" she demanded. "It's almost Christmas."

Neil shrugged. All the excitement he'd been feeling about Christmas had evaporated. Holly and Alex would never be together now — and there was nothing Neil could do about it.

Neil woke early on Christmas Eve morning. He lay staring up at his bedroom ceiling, trying to recapture the Christmas spirit he'd felt at Santaland, but images of Holly and of Alex's tear-streaked face kept crowding into his head.

He decided to get up and take Jake for a run. As usual, the Border collie was eager to go out, so the two of them set off for the ridge.

The ground was still thick with snow and the rising sun set it sparkling as if it was scattered with diamonds. It was a fantastic morning, but Neil couldn't enjoy it — not while his head ached with the misery of knowing Holly and Alex were parted forever.

Neil let Jake off the leash and watched him race back and forth, throwing up clouds of loose snow at every step.

They climbed steadily. By the time they reached the top of the hill, the sun was up and Compton lay below them, the snowy roofs and gardens looking strangely out of place against the brilliant blue sky behind.

A figure appeared on a path a little way ahead. Neil recognized her and his heart sank. He'd come here to try to forget about Alex for a while and here she was, walking slowly toward him.

Alex glanced up and saw him. She looked pale and miserable. "Sorry about yesterday," she said.

"How are you feeling?" Neil asked.

She shrugged. "Pretty awful, actually. But I know it was my own fault. . . . Look, I really can't stop and talk — Mom and Dad will be wondering where I am." She turned away. "Have a good Christmas."

Neil watched her walk away from him, head down and shoulders drooping. He wished there was something he could do or say that would cheer her up. But he knew it was hopeless.

"Neil!" Emily was dashing up the hill toward him.

"What's wrong?" Neil called.

"Nothing. Well . . . I don't know. Mom and Dad sent me to get Alex," Emily said.

"Why?" asked Neil.

"They wouldn't say," said Emily. "But they looked pretty pleased."

Neil shook his head. "I can't imagine what they could do to cheer her up. I've just seen her and she looks really upset."

"Well, you never know. Go and get her — and hurry up!"

"OK," Neil agreed reluctantly. He caught up with Alex near the path that led to her street. "Wait!" he called.

Alex turned.

"You've got to come to the kennels with me. Mom and Dad need to see you."

"I expect they want me to look at another dog." Alex shook her head. "It's kind of them but I'm not interested." She turned to go.

"Please," Neil said, catching her arm. "They wouldn't have sent Emily to find you if it wasn't important."

Alex shrugged. "OK. But it's a waste of time."

They hurried down to the kennels. Carole and Bob were waiting for them in the kitchen. "What's going on?" Neil asked. He got a towel and rubbed Jake's fur dry.

"You'll see." Bob winked at him, then placed a

plate of hot, buttered toast on the table. "Have some toast while you're waiting."

Just then Neil heard a car drive up. Carole ran to the front door and opened it. "They're here!" she cried.

"Who's here?" Neil demanded, standing up.

"Just wait and see," said Bob.

Neil glanced at Emily, hoping she could explain what was going on, but she looked just as confused as he felt. They heard Carole inviting somebody to come inside, then a dog's claws clicking along the hall. A moment later, Holly scampered into the kitchen, her tail wagging wildly. She spotted Alex and darted straight to her. Alex stared at the Labrador, her face clouded with uncertainty.

Holly jumped up and Alex bent down to pet her.

"What's going on?" Neil asked. "Why's Holly here?"

Carole came into the room with Mr. and Mrs. Biggs, the couple who had adopted Holly. "Mrs. Biggs phoned earlier," said Carole, "while you were out with Jake."

"That's right," Mr. Biggs said. "We took Topsy to the vet last night, and it turns out she's pregnant."

"Pregnant?" Neil repeated. "Of course! That's why she was looking so low."

"Yes, I suppose we should have thought of it before, really," said Mr. Biggs rather sheepishly.

Suddenly, Neil understood what this meant. "So, I suppose you can't really keep Holly now?" he asked tentatively, glancing across at Alex's hopeful face.

"Not really, no. We feel terrible about having to bring Holly back," Mrs. Biggs went on. "But we just won't be able to manage her when we've got a litter of pups, too. And when we called to explain what had happened, your mom told us that somebody else wanted Holly, anyway." She beamed at Alex. "I can see you're already very fond of her. And she obviously loves you."

Alex's eyes shone with joy. She swept the puppy into her arms and hugged her tightly. "Oh, Holly, I can hardly believe it," she cried. "Thank you for bringing her back. This is going to be the best Christmas ever!"

The Morgans and Holly came to King Street Kennels for Christmas dinner. As everyone sat down at the table, Neil looked around happily. It had turned out to be a perfect day.

He looked across the kitchen to where Bob was carving the turkey. Jake and Holly were sitting at his feet, watching hopefully in case he dropped a piece of meat. Mr. and Mrs. Morgan and Alex seemed happy and relaxed. Through the kitchen window, Neil could see snow falling gently.

"I'm glad you could all come today," Carole said. She filled everyone's glass. "As soon as Bob brings the turkey over, I think we should drink a toast."

They waited expectantly as Bob carefully carried the turkey to the table, stepping over the eager dogs.

Carole raised her glass of cider. "To Alex and Holly. It's great to see them back together again. And here's to a Merry Christmas to all of us."

Neil grinned as they clinked glasses. He looked down at Holly. She was leaning contentedly against Alex's leg, and Neil's smile broadened. For a while he had thought this Christmas would be terrible, but in the end it was turning out to be one of the best he'd ever had.